ALIENS, CREATURES & BEASTS

By Thomas Macri
Illustrated by Chris Kennett

 A GOLDEN BOOK • NEW YORK

ISBN 978-0-7364-3691-5
rhcbooks.com
Printed in the United States of America
10 9 8 7 6 5 4 3 2 1

A long time ago, in a galaxy far, far away . . .
there were different kinds of aliens who flew starships,
played in bands, and scavenged for junk. Some were even
Jedi and Sith—the most powerful warriors in the galaxy!

Ever wonder what these out-of-this-world beings were like? Well, get ready to learn all about the different aliens, creatures, and beasts of the *Star Wars* universe!

Some aliens were heroes!

Chewbacca was one of the greatest heroes in the galaxy. He fought alongside the Republic Army during the Clone Wars. He joined the Rebel Alliance's battle against Darth Vader and the evil Empire. And he helped the brave Resistance fight the First Order.

Chewbacca was a Wookiee from the forest planet Kashyyyk. He was covered in long brown fur and spoke in roars and groans. But his best friend, Han Solo, understood everything he said.

Chewie (as Han called him) was the copilot of the most famous starship in the galaxy, the *Millennium Falcon*!

Together, Chewbacca and Han blasted off into hyperspace to save the day many, many times.

Eventually, the young Resistance fighter Rey became the pilot of the *Falcon*. And loyal Chewbacca was by her side, continuing to fight for what was right.

Maz Kanata was over 1,000 years old when she helped the brave Resistance in their fight against the evil First Order. A small alien, Maz wore enormous goggles that helped her look deep into others' eyes to learn about them.

When Maz met the runaway stormtrooper Finn and the young scavenger Rey, she knew that they would both play important roles in the future of the galaxy.

The alien hero Jar Jar Binks was an amphibian, which meant he could live in water or on land. Jar Jar had a long, sticky tongue that he used to catch food.

When the Trade Federation's droid army attacked, Jar Jar fought to save Queen Amidala and the people of Naboo.

Two alien rebels helped steal the plans for the Empire's first Death Star.

Bistan was small but tough, and he was covered in fur!

Pao was a brave fighter with a very big mouth.

Rebel hero Admiral Ackbar was from the ocean planet Mon Cala. Ackbar led the Rebel fleet that destroyed both of the Galactic Empire's gigantic battle stations—the first and second Death Stars!

The admiral also helped the Resistance destroy the First Order's super-weapon, the Starkiller.

Some aliens were Jedi, guardians of peace and justice!

Yoda may have been short, but he was one of the mightiest and wisest aliens of all. Like all Jedi, Yoda got his power from the Force—an energy field created by all living things. And he was an expert with his laser-bladed sword, called a lightsaber.

Many of Yoda's fellow Jedi were aliens, too. Together, they defended the galaxy from the Sith—evil warriors who used the dark side of the Force to gain power and spread fear.

When the Empire tried to destroy the Jedi,
Yoda fled to the swamp planet Dagobah.
Many years later, he trained one of the
greatest Jedi ever known—Luke Skywalker.

Some aliens were downright evil! Darth Maul was a Sith warrior with black and red skin, yellow eyes, and sharp horns. This fierce fighter wielded a double-bladed red lightsaber. It took two powerful Jedi Knights—Qui-Gon Jinn and Obi-Wan Kenobi—to defeat him.

General Grievous led the droid army against the Republic during the Clone Wars. Although he looked like a droid, Grievous was really a cyborg—part alien and part machine. With robotic arms and legs, Grievous fought with four stolen lightsabers.

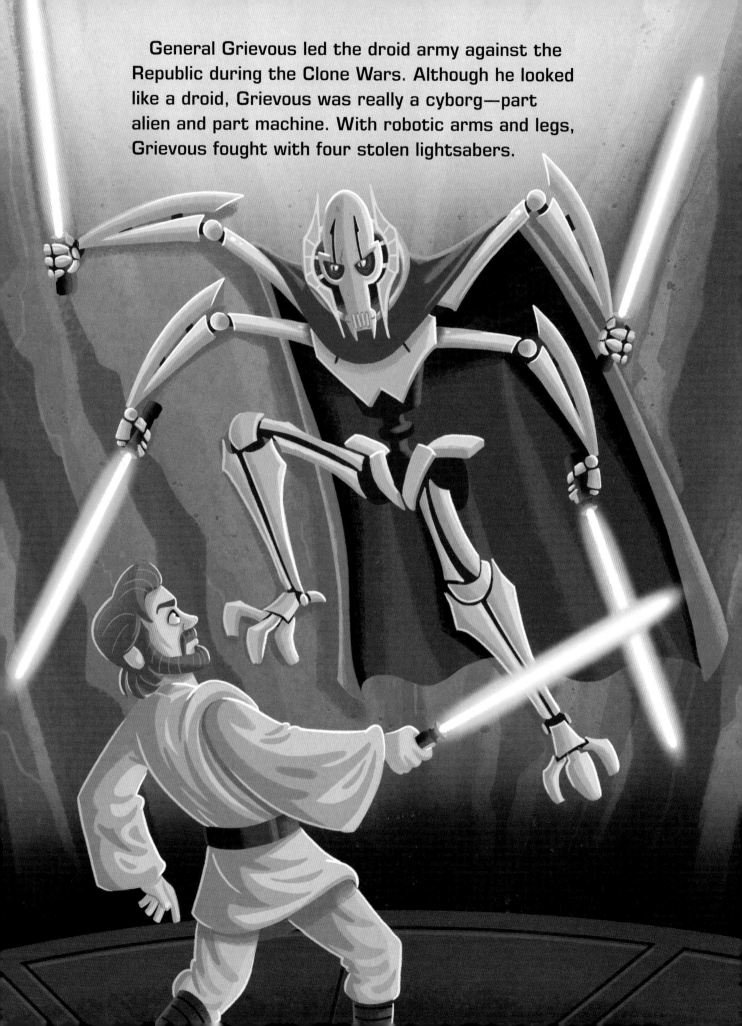

Some aliens were gangsters! Jabba the Hutt was the most powerful and feared crime lord in the entire galaxy. The huge slug-like creature's palace was filled with alien criminals who worked for him.

Bib Fortuna was a Twi'lek who managed Jabba's palace. He had piercing red eyes, fangs, and long tentacles protruding from his head.

Jabba's court jester was a cackling Kowakian
monkey-lizard named Salacious Crumb.

Hulking, pig-like Gamorrean guards protected Jabba.

When Han Solo owed Jabba money, the ruthless
gangster had the hero frozen in carbonite and hung
on his wall.

Some aliens were neither bad nor good—they simply worked for whoever paid them the most!

Zam Wessel was a bounty hunter who could change shape to look like anyone. This helped her hide when she was running from Jedi Knights Obi-Wan Kenobi and Anakin Skywalker.

Moroff was a Gigoran mercenary who sold his weapons, fighting skills, and brute strength to the highest bidder.

Greedo was a green-skinned Rodian with huge eyes and suction cups at his fingertips. He was hired by Jabba the Hutt to capture Han Solo—which turned out to be his last job.

With scaly skin and scary sharp teeth, Bossk was hired by Darth Vader to find the *Millennium Falcon*. But the bounty hunter Boba Fett beat him to it.

Some aliens lived in hot, dry deserts.

Jawas were tiny aliens who wore brown hooded robes. These timid scavengers traveled in huge vehicles called sandcrawlers. Jawas captured R2-D2 and C-3PO and sold them to Luke Skywalker and his uncle.

Tusken Raiders—also known as sand people—
wrapped themselves in cloth from head to toe.
These savage aliens would often attack strangers.
Poor Luke Skywalker learned this the hard way
when he set off to find R2-D2 after the droid
rolled away to find Obi-Wan Kenobi!

Some aliens lived in the freezing cold!
Tauntauns were two-legged animals with big flat feet, allowing them to run across snowy terrain.

Wampas were huge beasts with thick white fur to protect them from the cold and blend in with the snow. Their huge claws helped them catch prey.

While riding a tauntaun on patrol on the planet Hoth, rebel hero Luke Skywalker was attacked by a wampa! Luke was able to fight off the monster with his lightsaber.

Some aliens lived in the sea. The waters of the planet Naboo were filled with dangerous creatures.

The eel-like colo claw fish had many rows of sharp teeth and a glowing tail to lure prey.

The deadly opee sea killer hid in underwater rocks and caves. Its sticky tongue was big and strong enough to catch anything—including a submarine with Obi-Wan, Qui-Gon, and Jar Jar Binks inside!

Luckily, the gigantic sando aqua monster made a meal of the opee, allowing the heroes to escape.

Some aliens lived in the forest.

Ewoks were small, furry creatures—but don't let their cute looks fool you! They were fierce warriors who used weapons like wooden spears, stone catapults, and gliders.

Sometimes mistrustful of strangers, Ewoks captured rebel heroes Luke Skywalker, Han Solo, and Chewbacca. The droid C-3PO pretended he was a golden god and convinced the little aliens to set them free.

The brave Ewoks joined the Alliance in the fight against Imperial stormtroopers on their home planet, Endor. The rebels' furry new allies helped destroy the second Death Star—and defeat the Empire!

Some aliens were expert pilots!

Sebulba was a Podracer who won almost every race—because he always cheated! Only the young human Anakin Skywalker was able to beat him. A Dug from the planet Malastare, Sebulba had a long, scowling snout and walked on his arms.

With his huge black eyes, Nien Nunb helped the rebel general Lando Calrissian navigate the *Millennium Falcon* deep inside the second Death Star—and blow it up! Years later, Nien Nunb became an X-wing pilot for the Resistance.

Ello Asty was an X-wing pilot from the planet Abednedo. Ello helped the Resistance win an important victory against the First Order—the destruction of the Starkiller Base!

Everyone needs to have a little fun, even in the *Star Wars* universe, and these aliens were happy to provide it!

The Max Rebo Band filled Jabba the Hutt's palace with funky music. Their blue leader, Max, was a keyboardist. Droopy McCool played the chindinkalu flute with his big, powerful cheeks. And singer Sy Snootles had enormous lips at the end of a long, skinny snout.

Aliens in the Mos Eisley cantina would groove
to the tunes of Figrin D'an and the Modal Nodes.
This popular Bith band played strange instruments,
including the Kloo Horn and Double Jocimer.

Some aliens made a living with garbage!

Watto was a junk dealer who believed in only one thing—money! A Toydarian, Watto had wings, webbed feet, and a long snout. As a boy, Anakin Skywalker worked in Watto's junk shop—until Jedi Knight Qui-Gon Jinn flew him off Tatooine to train as a Jedi.

Teedos were small alien scavengers who rode on luggabeasts. One Teedo captured the Resistance droid BB-8 and tried to sell him. Luckily for BB-8, the young scavenger Rey set him free.

Unkar Plutt ran a junkyard at Niima Outpost on Jakku. Unkar bought junk from scavengers like Rey but never paid a fair price.

Some aliens actually made their homes in trash! The dianoga was a squid-like creature who lived in garbage compactors. It had one eye and tentacles to capture prey. The rebel heroes Luke Skywalker, Princess Leia, Han Solo, and Chewbacca encountered a hungry dianoga while trying to escape the first Death Star.

Some aliens spent their lives carrying things—or other aliens!

Eopies were four-legged pack animals from the planet Tatooine.

Tusken Raiders relied on aliens called banthas to get around. As Luke unfortunately found out on Tatooine, if you see banthas, Tusken Raiders are probably close by!

Rontos were the Jawas' favorite transport beasts.

Happabores were big and slow, but extremely strong and able to carry heavy loads. Finn learned the hard way that you shouldn't disturb them when they're thirsty!

When patrolling the deserts of Tatooine, Imperial stormtroopers rode on iguana-like dewbacks.

Varactyls were loyal lizard-like aliens with feathery manes. During the Clone Wars, Jedi Master Obi-Wan Kenobi rode a varactyl named Boga into battle against General Grievous and his droid army.

Some aliens were larger than life!

Exogorths were gigantic space slugs who lived inside asteroids. They were so big that they had bat-like aliens called mynocks living inside them!

When the crew of the *Millennium Falcon* was trying to escape the Empire, they hid inside an asteroid. Luckily, Han Solo realized that they weren't in a cave—but the belly of an exogorth! The *Falcon* zoomed safely away in the nick of time.

The Sarlacc was an enormous plant-like creature that digested its prey slowly over 1,000 years! Its body was buried underground, with only a beak and tendrils poking through to snare victims.

Jabba the Hutt tried to feed Han Solo and his friends to the Sarlacc on Tatooine. But the brave heroes defeated Jabba and sent his henchmen and Boba Fett tumbling down the Sarlacc's throat instead. *Burp!*

Some aliens were big, mean, and ugly! These vicious creatures were often caught and used as attack beasts.

When Padmé Amidala, Anakin Skywalker, and Obi-Wan Kenobi were captured by evil Count Dooku, the Republic heroes were forced to fight for their lives against three horrible monsters.

The acklay was an enormous predator with long, pointy claws to snap at victims—and razor-like jaws to chomp on them!

The nexu was a large catlike
creature with four eyes, sharp teeth,
and even sharper spikes and claws!

And the charging reek had four
strong legs and huge horns that
it used to ram its enemies.

Luckily, Yoda and the other Jedi
arrived just in time to save the heroes!

The rancor was a gigantic, mean brute with enormous claws and jaws. So it was no surprise that cruel Jabba the Hutt had a rancor as a pet . . . until Luke Skywalker crushed it under a blast door!

Rathtars were vicious creatures with a mouthful of sharp teeth and long tentacles to grab their victims. When rathtars got loose on Han Solo's freighter, they nearly made a meal of Rey and Finn!

In the *Star Wars* universe, aliens came in all different shapes, sizes, and colors. Some were good . . .

and some were evil.

Some were rich and powerful . . .

and others collected trash to survive.

But one thing was certain—the story of the galaxy wouldn't have been the same without them!